TABLE OF CONTENTS

Colorado Wildlife is Dedicated to:

ISBN 0-939650-13-4
ISBN 0-939650-12-6 (Pbk)

WELCOME

Where did we come from? How and when did life begin? Probably every person ever born has wondered about this. Are we relatives of the apes and reptiles? Did today's plants and animals start out millions and billions of years ago as simpler kinds of life? Evolutionists (ev-o-LOO-shun-ists) say yes. Creationists (kre-A-shun-ists) say no.

Creationists feel that God made every living thing by itself, out of nothing. Each new plant or animal was created much as you see it now, they say. It is not a relative of some earlier kind of life.

People have been arguing about Evolution for years. But the real blow-up came in 1859 when Charles Darwin wrote his book **The Origin of Species**. In this book, Mr. Darwin suggests that all living things started out long ago as simpler kinds of life. Scientists who agreed with Darwin said, "Look, we can show that fish came before amphibians, amphibians came before reptiles and reptiles came before people. Each kind of life changed a little bit, which made it possible for the next kind to come along."

Creationism and Evolution are **theories**: ideas or beliefs that help to answer a question or prove a point. Creationism and Evolution are two different ways of answering the question, "How and when did life begin?" But in **Colorado Wildlife** we do not talk about theories. Instead, we give you some of the history of life in Colorado, the history that we can see in fossils.

A writer for "Natural History" magazine says, "The results of history lie strewn around us." It's true. Right here in Colorado we can see stumps of ancient redwood trees, bones of early animals, insect fossils, dinosaur footprints.

Thread of Life, a new book about evolution, says "These truly are exciting times for anyone interested in the beauty and wonder of life on earth." Learning the history of plants and animals can only make life seem more amazing. Perhaps then, after reading about the history of life in Colorado, you will form your own theories. Or perhaps, like many people, you will still be left wondering, 'How and when **did** life begin?' Send us your ideas and theories:

Eleanor Ayer
JENDE-HAGAN BOOKCORP
P.O. Box 177
Frederick, CO 80530

LIFE COMES TO COLORADO

There was a time when nothing—no plant or animal—lived in Colorado; a time long before Colorado itself was a state or had a name. It was a time before the buffalo or the mammoth, even before the dinosaur, and **certainly** before man. It was a time too long ago for dates: hundreds of years or millions of years would be just little pinpoints on a time chart of the earth. This time before any life in Colorado was about 3-4½ BILLION years ago.

When did life begin in Colorado? It came so slowly that no one can put a date on it. For hundreds of thousands of years, there were only chemicals, mixing and bubbling together. Slowly, so slowly that it is hard to imagine, some very tiny bits of life formed from these chemicals, but nothing we would

People came on the earth about 2 million (2,000,000) years ago. But people have lived in Colorado only about 12 thousand (12,000) years. In Volume 3 of THE COLORADO CHRONICLES, *Indians of Colorado*, there is a time line on pages 2-3, showing how long people have lived in Colorado. If you wanted to put that time line on the end of this one, you would have to squeeze it down so small that it would be only a very thin part of the "Today" line. The whole 12,000 year time line of man in Colorado would be so thin you couldn't even see it!

know as plants or animals today.

Still, these tiny bits of life shared something with plants and animals of today. Something that was happening then is still happening now: **change.** Every plant and animal on the earth is made to live in the world around it. As the earth changes—the temperature, the water, the land, the air—so do the plants and animals. When certain kinds come on the earth that are **not** built to live here well, they die out. Plants and animals are still changing today, and they will keep changing forever as the earth changes or they, too, will die out.

About 600 million years ago, there were some things on the earth that we might know as plant or animal. These early kinds of life lived in the water. At first, many of them were just one cell, a cell being just about the smallest bit of life you can imagine. (People are made up of millions of cells.) Slowly they changed, until some plants and animals were made up of many cells. Some of the plants looked like corals do today. The animals had no backbones yet.

These animals living in the water changed over the next few million years into (as you might guess) fish. Fish of 375 million years ago were very different

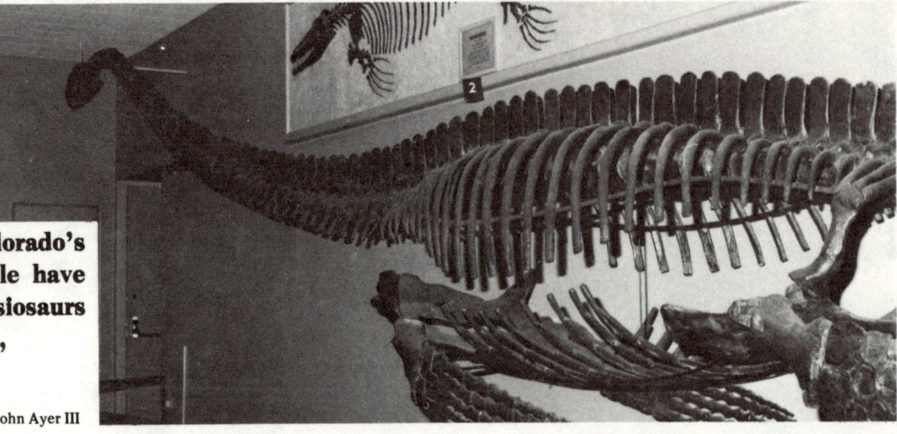

In southeastern Colorado's Baca County, people have found parts of plesiosaurs (PLEE-see-a-sawrs), lizard-like reptiles.

John Ayer III

from most of the ones we know today. But they had made an important change from earlier kinds of life before them: they had backbones. Fish have been changing ever since and they are still here more than 300 million years later. Many of today's fish are quite different from prehistoric kinds, but they're still fish!

Some of the first animals to move out of the water and onto the land were the scorpions. Moving onto the land was one of the biggest changes in all of animal history. By then, there were also plants that lived on the land. Huge forests began to grow that were filled with fern-like plants. In the water moved fish that looked like today's sharks. Insects were starting to buzz around. Cock-roaches, ants and mosquitoes had arrived! The date? About 250 million years ago.

This was the age of amphibians (am-FIB-e-uns): cold-blooded* animals with backbones and damp skin that lived in or near the water. Frogs and toads are some of today's amphibians. After the amphibians came the reptiles, who had dry, scaly skin. Some of today's reptiles are snakes and lizards, but 200 million years ago, you might have seen a hesperosuchus (hes-per-o-SOOK-us), a lizard-looking animal that could run very fast on its strong back legs.

In the Age of Reptiles, dinosaurs

were kings (and queens). Dinosaurs were some of the most amazing beasts that have ever roamed Colorado. They lived on earth for 120 million years. Much of what we know about dinosaurs has been learned right here in Colorado, for the beasts lived in many parts of our state.

During the next 60 million years, Colorado slowly changed from a warm, wet land to a cooler, dryer one. The great Age of Reptiles was coming to an end. Warm-blooded animals, smaller than most dinosaurs, came along. These animals began to look more like today's animals. Giant pigs, camels and rhinoceroses roamed around Colorado. Three-toed horses and other animals grazed in the tall grasses. At that point on the time chart, we were really quite close to today. The time then was just 12,000 years ago. There were people in Colorado! Near Greeley, men chased herds of mammoths. Soon, Indians would hunt buffalo. But before we get **too** modern, let's go back a hundred million years to the Dinosaur Age. We'll travel to western Colorado, near what will someday be the Utah border and see who was living in our state way back then.

---

*Cold-blooded animals: those whose bodies take on the temperature of the air or water around them, instead of keeping nearly the same temperature all the time, like warm-blooded animals do. Reptiles, amphibians and fish are cold-blooded. Birds and mammals are warm-blooded.

POINTS TO PONDER

1. You can make the time chart on page 2-3 really come alive by visiting the Colorado National Monument near Grand Junction. Starting on the floor of the canyon, you can see earth's history by looking at the different layers of rock. Much of the land here was built during the Age of Dinosaurs. In the early 1900's, not far from the park, scientists found the bones of one of the biggest dinosaurs ever known. You can get a free flyer when you write or visit the park:

Colorado National Monument
Fruita, CO 81521   (303) 858-3617

2. There is a fine natural history museum at the University of Colorado in Boulder. One of the things you can see there is a "History of the Earth" time chart which takes up one whole wall! Write for a free museum flyer or call to see when you can visit:

University of Colorado Museum
Henderson Building/Campus Box 218
Boulder, CO 80309   (303) 492-6165 or 492-6892

3. **Colorado in Millions and Billions**: How big **REALLY** is a million or a billion?

*Say you live in Durango and your father's company makes rulers. You decide to take one-foot (12″) rulers and lay them end to end until you have a billion. How far will you get? To Denver? To New York? No, you will get almost to the moon!

*Pretend your name is Atlas and you like to move mountains. You decide to take all the 14,000' peaks in Colorado and stack them on top of each other until you get a mountain a million feet high. How many of Colorado's 54 peaks will you need? Sorry, Atlas! You'll have to borrow some from other states. When you have all 54 stacked up, you will still need about half your pile again to reach a million feet!

*Suppose you are a ticket seller at Red Rocks Park near Denver. There's a big concert coming up and you plan to sell out all 12,000 seats at $1.00 per ticket. You'll collect $12,000! Now, if you can do that EVERY SINGLE NIGHT FOR 27½ YEARS, you'll collect about $120,000,000 (120 million dollars).....a dollar for each year that year that dinosaurs lived in Colorado!

4. **READ ON** About Colorado's early life. See if your library has these books:

1000 Million Years on the Colorado Plateau, by Al Look

Rim of Time, by Stephen Trimble

The World We Live In, by Time-Life Books

Exploring Rocks, Minerals and Fossils in Colorado, by Richard M. Pearl

THE TERRIBLE LIZARDS

His brain was the size of a golf ball—very small for a body so huge! He walked on all fours, his long back legs and short front legs always making him look off balance. The tiny head with the long beak nose held no teeth; he didn't really need any to chew the soft plants he ate. But oh, what would scare you the most if you saw this creature today would be the double row of pointed plates that ran down his 20-foot long back. Where the plates ended at the tip of his long tail, were four huge spikes which could kill almost any enemy.

This fierce creature didn't live on another planet. He lived right here in Colorado about 140 million years ago. His name: Stegosaurus (steg-o-SAWR-us), which means "plated lizard." Stegosaurus was not the biggest dinosaur that ever lived in Colorado, but he may have been the strangest looking. In spite of his fierce looks, though, he was really quite a peaceful animal.

Diplodocus (d-PLOD-a-kuss) was the longest Colorado dinosaur. In fact, diplodocus was the longest land animal that ever lived anywhere! The longest ones were nearly 80 feet—almost as long as three buses put end-to-end. This animal's head was so small and his body so big that it is a wonder he could ever get enought to eat! Diplodocus could move on the land if he had to, but more likely he lived in the water. It's just a lot easier to move 30 tons around in the water than it is on the land!

Dinosaurs were very different animals than we have in Colorado today. But Colorado itself was much different 100-200 million years ago. Instead of the dry air and cold winters we know today, Colorado in the Dinosaur Age was warm and wet. It was a swampy place with many rivers. Our Rocky Mountains were not yet here! In fact, where Snowmass Mountain is today, near

John Ayer III

Dinosaurs didn't worry much about state borders. Bones of many different kinds of animals have been found very near Colorado, if not right in the state. A skeleton of tyrannosaurus rex (ti-ran-o-SAWR-us; rex means 'king') was found in Montana. This animal was the fiercest of the meat-eating dinosaurs and he walked upright on his two back legs. A tall man would not have come up to the knee of tyrannosaurus! Western Kansas has fossils of prehistoric fish and turtles, left from a time when great seas and lakes covered this area.

Aspen, a fossil of a fish was found which had lived there 150 million years ago. From this fossil, scientists could tell that there was once a giant lake or sea where the ski area is today.

The trees and plants of 140 million years ago were very different from ones in Colorado today. The land then was much greener. Trees like you might find in the jungle today, then grew in Colorado. Some were 150 feet high! There were many ferns and mosses, but very few flowers and no cactus.

How do we know so much about plants and animals that lived so long ago? From fossils: bones, prints and other remains that have been well-kept in the earth for millions of years. One of the best dinosaur fossil beds in the world stretches across the border of Colorado and Utah. Bones were first found here at Dinosaur National Monument in 1909. Since that time, fossils of more than 300 animals (14 different kinds of dinosaurs) have been found here. Parts of prehistoric turtles and crocodiles are here, too.

At Dinosaur National Monument is buried the largest group of dinosaur bones in the world. But there are other places in the state where we can find bones from 100 million years ago. In Fremont County, near Canon City, parts of the stegosaurus have been found. In southeastern Colorado lived cretaceous (kr-TA-shus) fish. Cretaceous means 'like chalk.' At this time in history (about 100 million years ago) huge beds of chalk were being laid down in the western U.S. The fish that lived during this time were called cretaceous because the land around them was like chalk, not because they were chalk-like themselves!

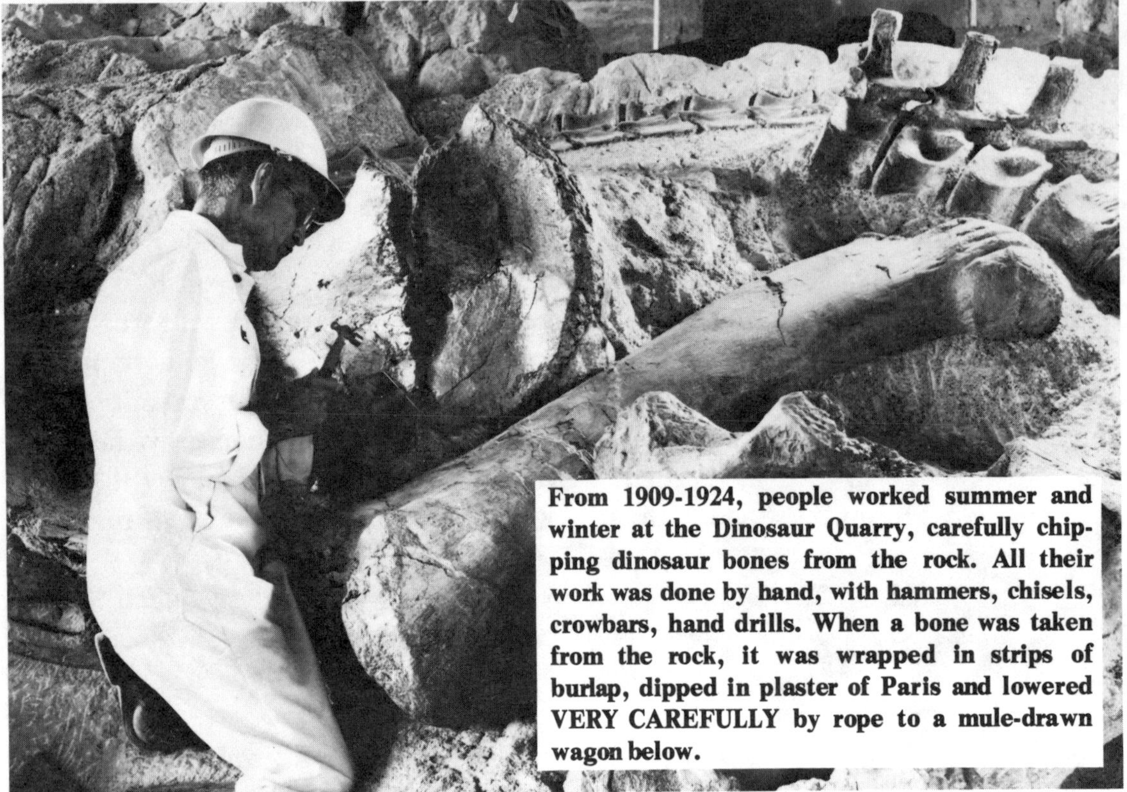

U.S. Department of Interior, National Park Service

But about 60-70 million years ago, these great Colorado creatures and millions like them began to die off. Fewer and fewer baby dinosaurs were born until at last there were no more of the beasts. Why did they die off? Scientists are not quite sure. Probably the changing earth—different temperatures and weather, different plants and animals—made it harder and harder for the dinosaurs to live here. The new dinosaurs being born were not made to live in this changing world and so they became extinct.

On April 28, 1982, Governor Lamm made the stegosaurus Colorado's official state fossil. For three years, students at McElwain Elementary School in Thornton had been pushing for stegosaurus to be added to the list of state symbols.

Margaret Malsam

POINTS TO PONDER

1. Maybe you're wondering why so many bones have been found near Dinosaur National Monument. Scientists think the bones were carried here by the river. You can find out for yourself from a scientist or guide when you visit Dinosaur National Monument. You can walk through a building where one whole wall is rock, with dinosaur bones still in place! Call or write for a flyer about this National Monument.

Dinosaur National Monument
P.O. Box 210
Dinosaur, CO 81610   (303) 374-2216

2. Dinosaurs are often called "The Terrible Lizards." But they really weren't terrible and they really weren't lizards. Some were as small as today's animals. Many were plant eaters, not like the fierce, flesh eating beasts you see in movies. Dinosaurs were able to live on the earth for 120 million years; people have been here only 1-2 million! You can learn a lot more about dinosaurs around the world by looking in these easy-to-read books:

Dinosaurs (A Little Golden Book) by Kathleen Daly

Let's Draw Dinosaurs, by Ann Davidow-Goodman

Dinosaurs (A Pictureback Book) by Peter Zallinger

Dinosaur Funbook, by William Johnson

The Warm-Blooded Dinosaurs, by Julian May

An Educational Coloring Book of Dinosaurs, Edited by Linda Spizzirri

3. While you're at the Denver Museum of Natural History, looking at diplodocus, stegosaurus and the rest, stop in the gift shop. There you will find dinosaur kits! Yes, you can build your own model dinosaur, any one of many different kinds.

4. Did you know you can go dinosaur tracking right near Denver? East of Morrison, just before you get to the Soda Lakes Road on Colorado Hwy. 8, you'll see some rock cliffs. In those rocks (and they're not hard to see) are honest-to-goodness dinosaur footprints!

5. READ ON About Colorado's Dinosaurs. See if your library has these books:

Dinosaur National Monument: The Story Behind the Scenery, by Allen Hagood

Dinosaur National Monument, by J. S. McIntosh

The Dinosaur Quarry, by Good, White and Stucker

1000 Million Years on the Colorado Plateau, by Al Look, chapter 5

FISH, AMPHIBIANS AND REPTILES

The men just leaned on their hands and knees, staring into the soft sandstone. For weeks, they had been camped near Canon City, digging, moving rocks and studying what they found. Until today, they hadn't found much, but now they knew they were onto something big.

At last, the leader of the group spoke. "Gentlemen, what you see before you, if I am not mistaken, is a piece of a plate that covered one of our ancient fishes. The bony plate was like armor: it protected the fish. Just how old this fish might be, I cannot say. We must study it further."

The year was 1893. What Charles D. Walcott and his scientists had found was the bony plate from the oldest kind of fish ever to live on earth! These fish lived 400 million years ago and are the oldest known animals with backbones. As strange as these armored fish must have looked, with their big bony plates, they were relatives of today's fish.

Over millions of years, fish changed, some becoming the kinds of fish we know today. Many of the lakes and oceans that once covered the earth began to dry up. To live in this new world, some kinds of fish developed lungs. With lungs, these new animals could breathe air, instead of having to breathe water through gills. Being able to breathe air, they could live outside the water. These were the earliest amphibians (am-FIB-e-uns): cold-blooded animals with backbones and a wet, smooth skin. Amphibians needed to live **near** the water but they did not need to live **in** it as fish did.

The earth kept getting drier and a new group of animals came along: reptiles. Reptiles were much better able to live on the land. Like amphibians and fish, they were cold-blooded and had backbones, but their skins were dry and scaly. They did not **have** to live in or near the water to keep their skin wet. Reptiles could lay their eggs on the land. Fish and amphibians had to lay theirs in the water.

Many ancient fish, amphibians and reptiles are extinct. Some did slowly change and are able to live in today's world. There are now 40,000 different kinds of fish! Some of today's amphibians that you might know are frogs and toads. Snakes are our best-known reptiles. Let's see which of these animals live in Colorado today.

Of the 40,000 different kinds of fish in the world, Colorado has 89. Many are natives. Some have been brought (or "introduced") to our state by the Colorado Division of Wildlife.

Like all animals, fish can be put into groups or families. Colorado fish fit into 16 different families. Half of those are fish that make good food and are often caught by fishermen. (Look in the pond at the bottom of this page). The other eight families are either not good to eat or are too rare to be caught. Let's look at those kinds first:

HERRINGS—Only one kind of herring in Colorado—the gizzard shad. Gizzard shad is eaten by other fish more useful to man, like the ones in the pond below.

MINNOWS—Often used as bait by fishermen to catch other fish. One kind, the Colorado squawfish, is the largest minnow in this part of the world. Another kind, carp, is caught and eaten by many people.

EELS—Look more like snakes than fish.

KILLIFISH—A common kind of fish, very good for aquariums.

LIVEBEARERS—Babies are born alive, like people, instead of being hatched from eggs like most other fish.

DRUM—Drum "grow their own food." The tiny animals that they eat must first hitch themselves onto the drum's body and grow before they are ready to be eaten.

SCULPINS—Found in mountain streams in western Colorado. Live in higher waters than any other Colorado fish.

SUCKERS—Some people fish for suckers. The meat tastes good, but there are many bones. Suckers are "bottom feeders": they find their food at the bottom of the water. Bottom feeders often eat a lot of dirt and garbage.

WHAT TO HOPE FOR ON THE END OF YOUR LINE

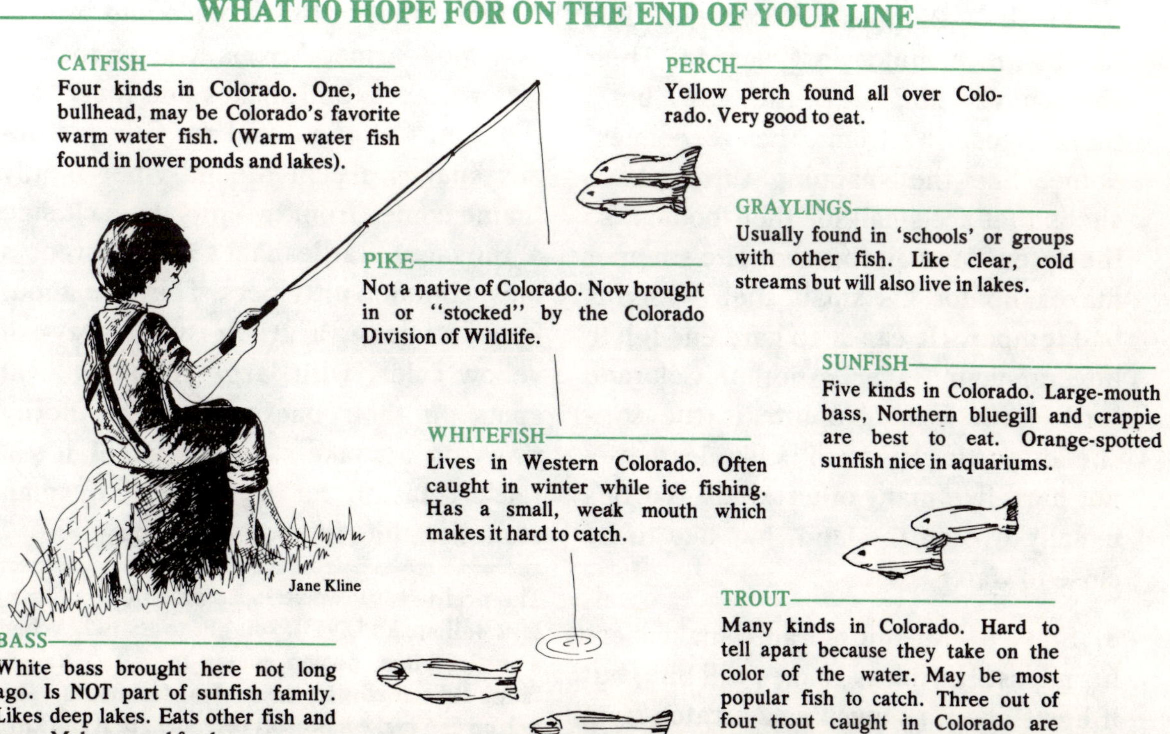

CATFISH
Four kinds in Colorado. One, the bullhead, may be Colorado's favorite warm water fish. (Warm water fish found in lower ponds and lakes).

PERCH
Yellow perch found all over Colorado. Very good to eat.

PIKE
Not a native of Colorado. Now brought in or "stocked" by the Colorado Division of Wildlife.

GRAYLINGS
Usually found in 'schools' or groups with other fish. Like clear, cold streams but will also live in lakes.

WHITEFISH
Lives in Western Colorado. Often caught in winter while ice fishing. Has a small, weak mouth which makes it hard to catch.

SUNFISH
Five kinds in Colorado. Large-mouth bass, Northern bluegill and crappie are best to eat. Orange-spotted sunfish nice in aquariums.

BASS
White bass brought here not long ago. Is NOT part of sunfish family. Likes deep lakes. Eats other fish and bugs. Makes a good food.

TROUT
Many kinds in Colorado. Hard to tell apart because they take on the color of the water. May be most popular fish to catch. Three out of four trout caught in Colorado are rainbow. Only native is cutthroat.

Jane Kline

AMPHIBIANS

Amphibians live in cool, wet places. So Colorado, with its dry and often hot air is not their favorite home! We do have two main kinds of amphibians: 1) Salamanders. 2) Frogs and Toads.

Salamanders—Often called "mud puppies." Only one kind in Colorado, but found nearly everywhere in the state. A dark color—nearly black, with yellow spots or stripes. Sometimes mistaken for a lizard. Salamanders are harmless.

Frogs and Toads—Many different kinds in Colorado. Which is which? Look behind the head. If you find a big swelling on each side, you have a toad. If you find no swellings, you have a frog.

REPTILES

By James vanRensselear

Out in the desert
Where the sands are hot
The lizards don't walk—
They gallop or trot.

And you would, too;
For it ain't so sweet
To have the old sand
A-burning your feet.

Oh, a lizard's feet
Is tender things,
And it wouldn't of hurt God
To give 'em all wings!

There are three kinds of reptiles in Colorado:

1) Lizards—Live in hot, dry places. Most Colorado lizards live around the edges of the state; very few in the mountains. No Colorado lizards are poisonous but some have a very painful bite. The skin of some is very brightly colored: if the male lizards have bright-colored skin, the females don't. If the female has pretty skin, the male doesn't.

2) Turtles—Reptiles with shells. Box turtles are common in Colorado. Their shells have "hinges" so they can "box" themselves in from their enemies. Some, like the snapping turtle, have shells that are small for their bodies, so they aren't as well covered. The snapper makes up for his small shell with his bad temper. He can snap hard enough to bite off your finger! Another Colorado turtle with a terrible bite is the soft-shelled turtle. His shell is like leather—not hard like many other kinds. Turtles usually live on the land, but like to be close to water.

3) Snakes—Most Colorado snakes are harmless. Harmless snakes will bite, but it hurts about as much as a scratch from a rosebush. Snakes are a great help to farmers: they eat rats, mice and insects that spoil farmers' crops. Garter snakes, water snakes, bull snakes and racers are common Colorado snakes. Our poisonous snakes are in the pit-viper family (name comes from two pits on each side of the face). Rattlesnakes are Colorado's most common pit-vipers. They are about four feet long, a green-ish or gray-ish yellow color, with large round or oval spots on their backs. Look for horny rings on a snake's tail to tell if it's a rattler. Listen for a sound like small stones rattling in a wooden box.

The prairie rattlesnake looks much like a harmless bull snake UNTIL you get to its tail. When a rattler bites, poison comes from two hollow fangs (like teeth) in the roof of its mouth. The poison can make a person very sick, or it can kill.

POINTS TO PONDER

1. SNAKES ALIVE! is a show at the Denver Museum of Natural History. You can see pictures of Colorado snakes and hear people talk about them. But best of all, you can hold and pet some non-poisonous kinds! To find out more about SNAKES ALIVE! call the Public Relations Office at the Museum: (303) 322-1302.

2. Do you like to fish? The Colorado Division of Wildlife can sell you a fishing license, tell you about good fishing spots, or give you some fishing tips. They have posters, flyers, books and even a magazine which will help you learn more about Colorado fish. In Denver, call or write: Colorado Division of Wildlife; 6060 Broadway; Denver, CO 80206   (303) 297-1192

There are also offices in Fort Collins, Colorado Springs, Grand Junction, Montrose and Pueblo.

3. If you live near Colorado Springs, the Bear Creek Nature Center is a fun place. There you can watch salamanders, snakes, toads, turtles and other Colorado creatures. You can even help catch their food and feed them! Call the Nature Center at (303) 471-KIDS.

4. Did You Know…….

*Snakes don't chew their food; they swallow it whole!

*The biggest trout caught in Colorado weighed 36 pounds and was 3½ feet long!

*When they're caught, lizards can break off their tails to get away. (Later, they grow new ones!)

*Yellow mud turtles give off a bad smell when they are touched. This has given them the name of ''stinkpot'' or ''stinking-jim!''

*Some frogs and toads live in trees and are called tree toads or tree frogs. Colorado has tree frogs (but they are most often found on the ground!)

*Snakes shed by turning their skins inside out. As they crawl out of their old skin, even the film that covered their eyes comes off! Some kinds shed many times a year. Every time a rattlesnake sheds, it adds another rattle to its tail!

5. READ ON About Colorado's Reptiles, Amphibians and Fish. See if your library has these books:

Amphibians and Reptiles in Colorado, by G. A. Hammerson

A Family Guide to Warm Water Fishing, by John W. Malo

Game Fish of Colorado, by John Woodling

Guide to the Amphibia of Colorado, by Hugo Rodeck

Guide to the Fishes of Colorado, by W. C. Beckman

Guide to the Lizards of Colorado, by T. Paul Maslin

Guide to the Snakes of Colorado, by W. H. Jones-Burdick

Guide to the Turtles of Colorado, by Hugo Rodeck

ECOLOGY AND LIFE ZONES

How often do you see wild bighorn sheep in Denver? Or aspen trees at the top of Pikes Peak? Or sagebrush in Breckenridge? Or a white-tailed ptarmigan on the eastern plains? Never, of course!

You learn how and why different plants and animals live where they do, when you study ecology (e-KOL-o-gee). Some people who study Colorado ecology divide the state into five groups or "life zones." Each zone is higher than the zone below. With each new zone comes a change in the air, land and water. As the zones change, the plants and animals change, too.

Now of course there isn't a fence around each zone to keep animals and plants in the right places. Some animals live in one zone in the summer and move to another in the winter. Some plants and animals live in more than one zone. But often, a plant or animal has one zone that is just right, one place where you most often find it. We call this place the plant or animal's habitat: the area where it lives best.

Nature is always working to stay in balance, to keep the habitat just right for each kind of life. If a stream gets warmer or colder, even just a little, it can change life for all the plants and animals around it. Some will be able to live with the new temperature. Others will die. Some of the fish might move to another stream. With their food changing or gone, life will be different for the animals who live around the stream.

When nature makes changes in a habitat, they are usually slow. They may take hundreds or thousands or millions of years. Nature gives the plants and animals time to change. But when man changes a habitat—by poisoning or polluting or just plain moving in—the changes happen fast: within months or weeks or days. The plants and animals don't always have time to change and nature's great balance is tipped. Of course not all man-made changes are bad. Scientists and wildlife workers have been able to save some kinds of plants and animals that might have died out. But often, man's changes are made too fast, without thinking about the whole of ecology.

As you read on about Colorado wildlife, look back to the Life Zone Chart. Which kinds of animals live in the same zones? What kinds of plants live with them? Is it warm or cold there? Wet or dry? Think about nature's great balance and how easily it can be tipped if changes happen too fast.

COLORADO'S LIFE ZONES

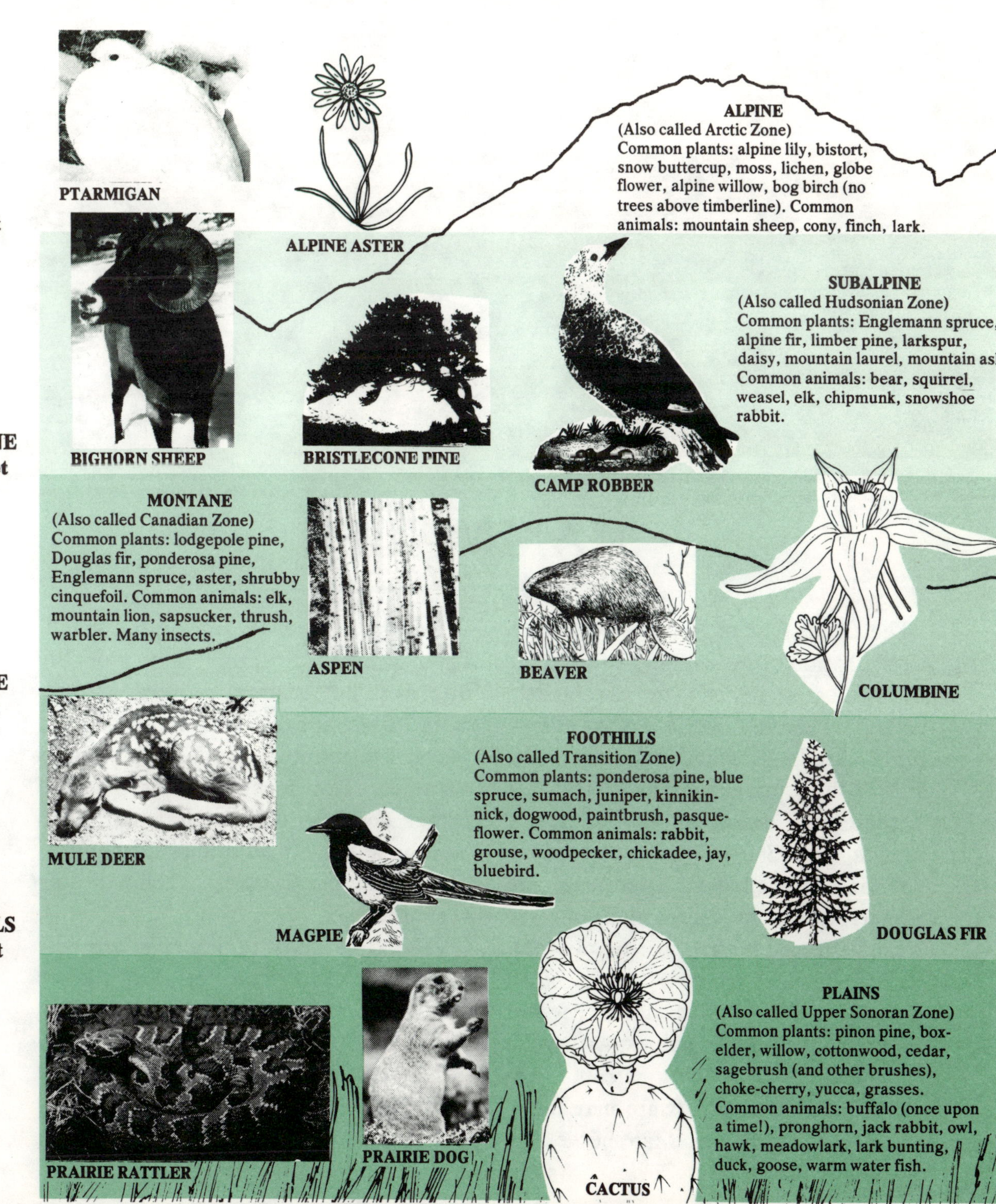

Early Age of Mammals in the Rocky Mountains

MAMMALS

The Great Age of Reptiles was over. After 120 million years, only a few kinds of reptiles were left on the earth: turtles, lizards, snakes, crocodiles. A new kind of animal had taken the place of the reptiles: **mammals**. The Age of Mammals began about 60 million years ago, and it is still going on today.

What are mammals? Mammals are animals that have backbones and are usually covered with fur or hair. Mammals are warm-blooded (their blood stays at the same temperature). Mother mammals feed their babies with milk from their own bodies. People are mammals. Dogs and cats are mammals. Whales are mammals. Mammoths and mastadons were also Colorado mammals, but they are now extinct.

The first mammals were quite small. Their brains were tiny and probably they were not as smart as today's mammals. But slowly, over thousands of years, the different kinds of mammals changed. The legs of some became longer so they could run faster. The mouths and teeth of others changed to help them chew better. Their brains became larger.

Very few kinds of animals are left today in Colorado from the early Age of Mammals. But by 35 million years ago, there were mammals on earth that we might know today. Rhinoceroses roamed the Great Plains. Camels lived in Colorado way back then! There was even a prehistoric horse, smaller than today's horse.

But then, just before people came to Colorado, something happened. Maybe it was a great disease. Maybe the earth itself changed too fast for the animals. In just a short time, many of these mammals were extinct in Colorado. Luckily, some of the horses, rhinoceroses, camels and other mammals moved north toward Alaska and crossed into Asia. (At that time, a land "bridge" still connected Asia and Alaska.) Because they moved and did not become extinct, they live today in other parts of the world. One of these mammals, the horse, came back to Colorado with the Spanish, thousands of years later.

Many kinds of mammals that were here when people came to Colorado 12,000 years ago are still here today. Let's look at today's mammals in three groups. In each of these groups, there are different families, but all the families are alike in a few ways:

Colorado's Meat Eating Mammals

* Name (carnivore) means "flesh-eating;" often kill other animals for food
* Because they hunt other animals, they're called "predators;" very important to balance of nature
* Not all "meat-eaters" eat just meat; some eat plants, too
* Meat-eaters some of the smartest animals
* Often choose one place to live, instead of roaming in herds
* 274 kinds of meat-eating mammals around the world

BLACK BEAR

BEAR FAMILY: Grizzly & Black Bears
* Very few, if any, grizzly bears left in Colorado
* "Black" bear can also be cinnamon or brown
* Bears sleep many weeks in winter
* Like to be alone, away from other bears or people
* Black bears weigh 300-400 pounds; but a grizzly can weigh much more

DOG FAMILY: Coyotes, Wolves & Foxes
* Coyote is a sly, clever, curious animal
* Indians say coyote will be the last animal on earth
* Coyotes often hunted by ranchers who fear they will kill sheep and other animals
* Wolf nearly extinct in Colorado
* Four kinds of Colorado foxes: gray, red, kit, swift

COYOTE

MOUNTAIN LION

CAT FAMILY: Mountain Lion, Bobcat, Lynx
* Mountain lion also called puma
* Shy: rarely known to hurt a person in Colorado
* Hunters kill fewer than 100 a year here
* Mountain lion kills and eats deer
* Lynx rare in Colorado; probably any short-tailed wild cat found here is a bobcat
* Bobcat smaller than a lynx

WEASEL FAMILY: Weasel, Marten, Ferret, Wolverine, Mink, Otter, Badger, Skunk
* This family often puts out bad smell when scared
* Weasels have been called "blood-thirsty;" said to kill other animals even when they're not hungry
* Brown fur in summer; white (ermine) in winter. Weasel fur worth money. Once only kings and queens wore ermine
* Badgers are super diggers
* Small number of otters and wolverines in Colorado
* Ferret now extinct here

RACCOON

WEASEL

RACCOON FAMILY: Raccoon, Ringtail
* Raccoons are natives of every state in the U.S.
* Eat nearly everything; two favorites are green corn and watermelon
* Have black "masks" across their eyes
* Raccoon oil once used in Old West kitchens and to oil farm machines
* Ringtail has longer, bushier tail than raccoon

Colorado's Hoofed Mammals

* Have an even number of hoofed toes on each back foot
* Many have horns or antlers on their heads; antlers are shed (fall off) each year; most horns are not shed
* Most eat plants and roam the land in herds
* Some have stomachs with more than one part, so they can "chew their cuds"
* Male animals have many "wives"
* Besides Colorado's hoofed mammals, this group has pigs, cattle, giraffes, hippopotamuses, camels…more than 150 different kinds in all!
* Hoofed animals probably more useful to people than any other animals

BIGHORN SHEEP

* Made Colorado's state animal in 1961
* Mostly grayish-brown, with big white spot on rump
* Females have curved horns; males horns are curled tighter
* Live on high rocky cliffs
* Covered with hair, not wool
* 3-day-old lambs can follow their mothers across high cliffs
* Colorado and Wyoming have more bighorns than nearly any other states!

ROCKY MOUNTAIN GOAT

* Brought here in 1950's from nearby states
* Lives on very steep cliffs; can walk easily there without falling
* Has a beard on chin and hairy pants on front legs
* White coat of heavy, long, soft hair
* Very little goat hunting allowed in Colorado

* Most often hunted large animal in Colorado (about 50,000 killed a year)
* Name comes from its large ears, like a mule
* Males have antlers
* Speed, smell and hearing help them escape danger
* Colorblind: can see only black, white and gray
* May be more mule deer in Colorado than any other state!
* Baby deer (fawns) have white spots, as shown here

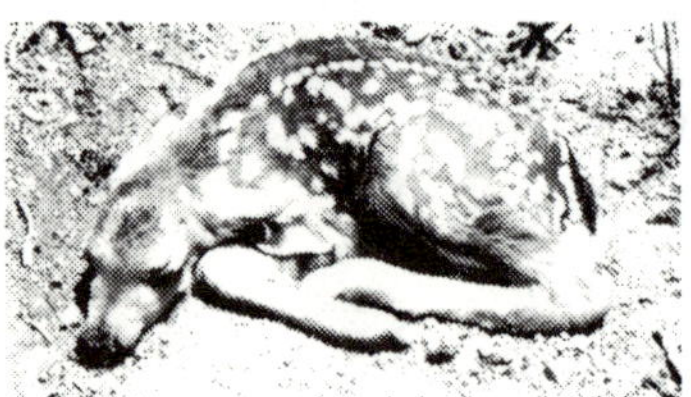

MULE DEER

* One of Colorado's largest animals: 400-1000 pounds
* Has white spot on rump like bighorn sheep
* Males sometimes make loud musical sounds to females called "bugling" (like sound of a bugle)
* Some Indians called elk "wapiti"
* People often collect elk's teeth; look like ivory
* Colorado has more elk than any other state except Wyoming

ELK

* Once were many million; now only 30,000 in Colorado
* One of fastest animals in the world, but usually will not jump a fence
* Has horns, but sheds them each year; white bands of fur on neck
* Likes to eat cactus flowers
* When scared, tightens muscles which raises white hair on rump and warns other animals of danger; also puts out special warning smell
* Sometimes called the "American Antelope" but is not really an antelope

PRONGHORN

* Not often thought of as a Colorado mammal; more often found farther north
* Can weigh 900-1400 pounds (half a ton!); babies can weigh 30 pounds when born
* Has scoop-like antlers six feet across
* Indian name means "twig-eater"
* Protected in Colorado: no moose hunting

MOOSE

* Someone's missing! One of the most important hoofed mammals in Colorado's history…
read the next chapter to find out who!

Photos from Colorado Historical Society and Colorado Division of Wildlife

Colorado's Rodents

*Rodents small in size but large in numbers: more than 2400 different kinds of rats and mice in the world
*Each has four big front teeth: two up and two down. Teeth are growing all the time; animals must gnaw every day to wear them down
*Wild rodents live closer to people than most other mammals
*Rodents VERY important to man, but in bad ways: carry diseases, kill crops, eat grain, cause flooding problems by the way they build, dig and tunnel

PRAIRIE DOG

SQUIRREL FAMILY: Chipmunks, Prairie dogs, Marmots, Ground Squirrels are in "Ground Squirrel Group;" Pine, Tuft-eared and Fox Squirrels in "Tree Squirrel Group"
* Prairie dogs "bark" when they're scared
* Prairie dogs live in "towns;" sit at doorway hole until they spot danger, then dive underground
* Prairie dogs found only in the West

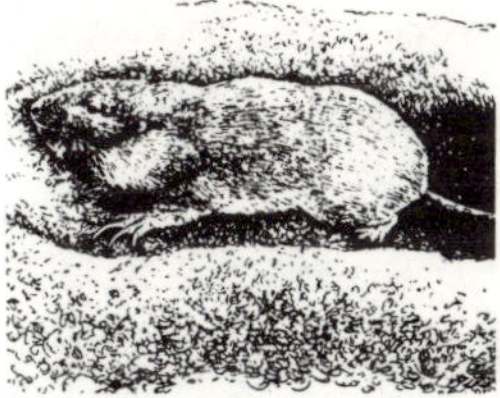

POCKET GOPHER

POCKET GOPHER FAMILY: Three different kinds in Colorado, but all called "pocket gophers" and hard to tell apart
* Live underground
* Loose pile of dirt in a field often shows a gopher hole
* Pocket gophers dig tunnels to get to plant roots for food
* Get the name "pocket" from fur-lined cheek pockets on each side of face

KANGAROO RAT

KANGAROO RAT & POCKET MICE FAMILY
* Like the pocket gopher family (above) in just one way: both families have "pockets" in their cheeks. Very different in most other ways
* Pocket gophers LOVE the underground; pocket rats and mice made for living above ground. Can run or leap over the ground very fast
* Kangaroo rats have long tails and back legs for leaping
* Have pouches on their fronts like the large kangaroos
* Kangaroo rats make very nice pets; seen most often at night

MUSKRAT

NATIVE RATS, MICE, VOLES, MUSKRATS: Many different kinds of rats and mice— meadow mice, cotton rats, deer mice, pack rats and more
* These "natives" were in Colorado long before people
* Some in the family have long tails and some have short
* The vole is a kind of meadow mouse
* Muskrat looks like a giant meadow mouse; tail is higher than it is wide; ears so small they're hard to see
*Muskrat lives near water; trapped for its skin

PORCUPINE

PORCUPINE FAMILY: No other animals in this family in the U.S.
* Quite different from other rodent families
* Live near trees, but sometimes found on the Plains
* Has about 30,000 quills which it **cannot** shoot
* Slightest touch of porcupine quill and it is yours!
* Slaps tail to send quills into enemy
* Likes to eat tree bark; can kill a tree by eating all the way around it
* Also called "quill pig"

* Someone's missing! One of the most important rodents in Colorado's history…
read the next chapter to find out who!

These are the three main groups of mammals in Colorado, but there are a few other mammals that don't really fit into these groups. One is the bat. You may think the bat is a bird because it flies, but it, too, is a mammal. Its "wings" are really made of skin, stretched between long, bony fingers. Bats fly at night and like to hang upside-down in caves or in trees during the day. (By the way, there are at least 17 different kinds of bats in Colorado, but no vampire bats!)

Moles and shrews are two other Colorado mammals. There are many kinds of shrews, but the water shrew is one of the smallest of all mammals. By trapping air bubbles in its fur, the water shrew can "run" across the top of the water. It needs to eat all the time and can starve to death in just a few hours if it does not have food. Moles are not often found in Colorado. They live underground and have eyes and ears that are almost too small to see. Moles move underground by "swimming" with their shovel-like front feet.

Marsupials (mar-SOO-pee-uls) are mammals that carry their babies in pouches on their bodies. Kangaroos are marsupials, but there are no kangaroos in Colorado. Our only marsupials are opossums. Opossums like to hang by their long, rat-like tails from tree branches, which makes it very handy for them to steal birds' eggs from nests. They also will "play possum" when scared: play dead so well that their enemies often just go away.

The rabbits-hares-pikas group could almost go on our rodent page. These animals all have big front teeth and chew on plants and trees, but they are not rodents. Hares (jackrabbits and snowshoes) live in nests on top of the ground. Rabbits (cottontails) live underground. Baby hares are born with all their fur and their eyes are wide open. Baby rabbits have no hair when they're born, and they cannot see. The cottontail is Colorado's most popular small animal for hunting. If you haven't been in Colorado's high mountains, you probably haven't seen a pika. These little creatures live above timberline. The pika is a relative of the rabbit, but it looks more like a mouse without a tail!

Now, think again about the missing hoofed animal and the missing rodent. These may have been the two most important wild animals in Colorado's history. Who were they? Read on to find their story!

John Ayer III

Huge animals once roamed the Plains in herds. The mammoth stood 14 feet high at his shoulders and had tusks (two long, pointed teeth) that weighed half a ton! Huge wild pigs once lived in Colorado. Saber-toothed tigers and giant ground sloths were here too.

POINTS TO PONDER

1. WHERE CAN I SEE WILD MAMMALS? To find a good spot close to you, call the National Forest Service (look in the phone book white pages under U.S. Government). They can give you maps and help you plan your trip. The Colorado Division of Wildlife prints a book called **Guide to Colorado's State Wildlife Areas** which lists 37 good places to animal-watch in Colorado.

2. WHERE CAN I SEE "WILD" MAMMALS IN THE CITY? In Denver, you'll want to go to the zoo in City Park. There you can see bighorn sheep, Rocky Mountain goats and more. In the Children's Zoo part, there is a prairie dog town. Call the zoo for times and costs: (303) 575-2754. Near NCAR in Boulder is a great place to watch elk, mule deer and bighorn sheep. The animals are most often here in winter when they come down from the higher mountains looking for food.

3. The "war" between man and coyote has been in the news a lot in the past few years. Look for these magazine stories in your library. After you have read them, ask yourself, "What would I do if I were a rancher worried about coyotes?"

"Call of the Wild," *Time* (August 10, 1981) Also look in the June 1, 1981 issue
"War on the Range: Sheep 1, Coyotes 0," *Newsweek* (November 8, 1982).
  Also look in the October 26, 1981 issue

"It's Hard to Keep This Predator Down," *National Wildlife* (Feb.-Mar., 1982)
"Crying Coyote," *Audubon* (March, 1982) Also look in September, 1982 issue

4. Rabbit Ears Pass, Wolf Creek Pass, Little Bear Peak, Deer Trail...all take their names from common Colorado mammals. But what about Molas Pass, Culebra Peak, Conejos, Toponas? What animals are these places named for? Where are they in Colorado? (If you need some clues, look in the book **Colorado Place Names** by Geo. R. Eichler.) Then make up another list of "stumpers" to try on your friends. There are many more!

5. READ ON About Colorado Mammals...See if your library has these books:

Game Animals of Colorado, by the Colorado Division of Wildlife

A Big Game Hunter's Guide to the Colorado Rockies, by S. N. Mazzone

Guide to the Mammals of Colorado, by Hugo Rodeck

Wildly Speaking, by M. B. Grant

Rocky Mountain Mammals, by David Armstrong

Rocky Mountain Wildlife, by Donald Blood

Wild Mammals of Colorado, by R. R. Lechleitner

Colorado Historical Society

BURRO, BEAVER AND BUFFALO

You know that old saying, 'A man's best friend is his dog'? Well I, for one, don't believe it. I'll tell you why. First, let me introduce myself. The name's Prunes. Miners up around Fairplay called me that 'cause they said my fur looked like dried fruit. They also called me (and all the rest of us burros) Rocky Mountain Canaries. Pokin' fun at us, they were, 'cause we had such awful voices when we "hee-hawed." Said we sounded about as far from a canary as you could get.

Well maybe so. And maybe my fur did look like prunes. But I can tell you this: no dog ever lived that was a better friend to man than us burros. The loads we hauled in and out of those mines! Tools, timbers to keep the mine roofs from caving in, even track for the railroads when they started using trains in the mines. Hauled all these things a-way back into those dark mines. Then, of course, we carried loads back out— buckets of rock usually, that the miners hoped had some gold to make them rich.

I worked most of my life in the gold mines around Alma and Fairplay. Hauled loads in and out of the mines all day. Lived in town with my owner, Rupe, an old miner. I had it pretty good, but I've heard that some of my burro buddies who worked in the coal mines never saw daylight their whole lives. They stayed underground in the mines from the time they were born 'till the time they died. You just name me a dog that would work like that! Nope…Colorado mining and Colorado history would never have been the same without us burros.

I have to say that we burros weren't

Colorado Historical Society

Full-grown beavers weigh about 40 pounds and can be as long as four feet. Their sharp, strong front teeth are great for 'biting down' trees. With the trees, they build houses and dams across streams, making their own little ponds.

the only animals who had a big part in Colorado history. Do you know what animal really started the rush to Colorado? The beaver—largest rodent in all of North America.

Before the white man came to our state about 1800, there were beaver everywhere, thousands and thousands of them. But about that time a new fad was starting back East and in Europe: beaver hats, hats made of beaver fur. To make these hats, companies needed more and more beaver skins. At first, they sent men out to trade with the Indians for skins, but soon the Indians couldn't trap beaver fast enough, so the white man came and trapped too.

The mountain men and fur trading lasted about 37 years, from 1806-1843. By the middle 1800's, beaver hats were ''out'' and silk hats were ''in.'' There wasn't the big need for beaver skins any more. It was probably a good thing, too, because beaver were getting harder and harder to find. The trappers had caught so many of them that they were ''endangered.'' About 1900, the government started ''protecting'' beaver— wouldn't let people trap them any more. Protecting beaver did help them stay alive. But people have changed Colorado's wild land so much in the last 100 years that we may never again have as many beaver as we once did.

Colorado Historical Society

Meet My Family—ASS: A wild animal that belongs to the horse family. DONKEY: An ass that has been tamed by man. BURRO: A small donkey. MULE: Cross between a female horse and a male donkey. HINNY: Cross between a male horse and a female donkey.

Now that's a sad story about the beaver. But there's another animal story in Colorado history that I think is even worse. It's the story of the buffalo.

Once, you see, there were 60 million buffalo roaming the Great Plains. They moved in groups called herds, always looking for food and water. Some of the paths they made are now roads across the U.S. The buffalo could go for days without water, which was a big help out on those dry, sunny plains. If there wasn't much water, the buffalo would drink water so dirty that other animals turned away. They lived well this way, with only one enemy (the wolf) until the white man came. The white man changed it all.

The Indians had hunted buffalo for many years. They ate buffalo, wore buffalo, made tools from buffalo and even burned buffalo dung to keep warm. From the Indians, the white man learned how to hunt buffalo. But sad to say, white men made a game of buffalo hunting. They didn't use the buffalo like the Indians did. Often, they just shot at the animals to see how many they could hit, then left them there to die and rot. Others shot the animals but took just the skins back East, where they sold them to be made into clothes for the rich. There were even stories that the white man was killing the buffalo to starve the Indians.

You can probably guess the end of the story. By 1865, two out of every three buffalo in America had been killed. By 1895, the buffalo was nearly extinct—gone forever. Just before it was too late, people saw what was happening. The government stepped in and put a stop to the buffalo killings, to keep the great beasts from becoming extinct. Today in Colorado, some ranchers raise buffalo, but they no longer roam free on the Great Plains.

These are just a few of the animals that have made history in Colorado. And you see—a dog hasn't been named once!

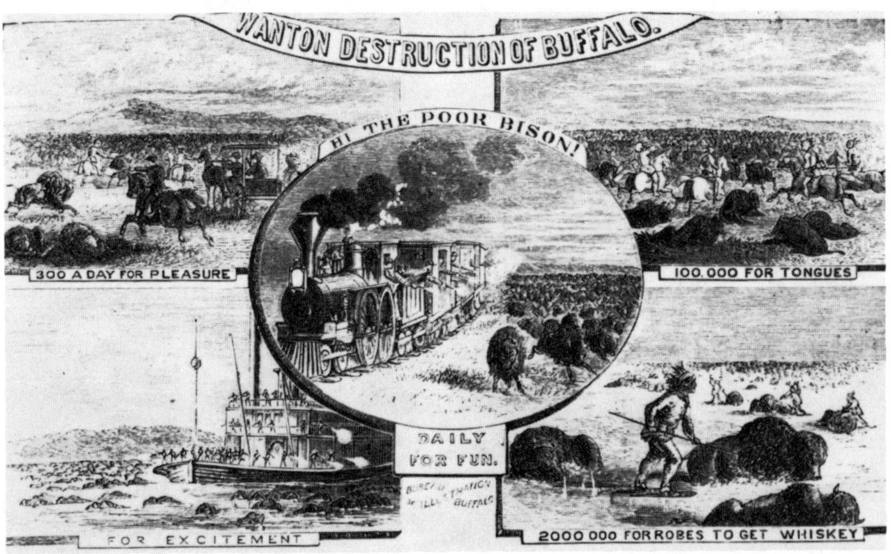

Colorado Historical Society

When the railroad was being built across the U.S., it was Buffalo Bill's job to get the meat to feed the workers. To do this, he killed more than 4,000 buffalo in 17 months. Buffalo tongues were a real taste treat; but what some hunters liked even better was the buffalo's hump!

Buffalo or bison? You've probably heard this animal called both. True BUFFALO live in Africa and Asia. Our American buffalo should be called by its right name—BISON. It's hard to change history though: *Bison* Bill?? The Indian *Bison* Nickel????

Colorado Division of Wildlife

POINTS TO PONDER

1. Just off I-70, about 20 miles east of Denver, you can watch and take pictures of buffalo. The place is Genessee Park, one of the Denver Mountain Parks. South of Denver about 20 miles, at Daniels Park, you can also watch the beasts roam.

2. As you read this and other wildlife books, watch for these words:

EXTINCT—Gone forever; when a kind of plant or animal has disappeared from the Earth.
ENDANGERED—In danger of becoming extinct.
THREATENED—May soon become endangered.
PROTECTED—"Cared for" by the government to be sure it does not become threatened, endangered or extinct. It is against the law to harm or kill a protected animal or plant.

3. This NBA has nothing to do with basketball. It's the National Buffalo Association—**THE** place to learn more about buffalo. The NBA prints a magazine called **Buffalo!** and has a free flyer which tells more about the group. Write or call: The National Buffalo Association; Box 706; Custer, SD 57730   (605) 673-2073

4. One of the finest zoos in the world is just west of Colorado Springs on Cheyenne Mountain. It's the Cheyenne Mountain Zoo, famous for the many kinds of animals that are born and raised right there. Call to find out more about the zoo: (303) 475-9555.

5. READ ON About Buffalo, Beaver and Burros. See if your library has these books:

The Beaver in Colorado, by W. H. Rutherford
Beavers, by James Poling
The Buffalo Book, by David Dary
Bison: The Great American Buffalo, by Lorence Bjorklund
Return of the Buffalo, by Jack D. Scott
Two Burros of Fairplay, by Caroline Bancroft
Wildlife in Danger, by the Colorado Division of Wildlife

ARTHROPOD FAMILY TREE

Jane Kline

BUGS (AND OTHER ARTHROPODS)

If you could bring together all the plants and animals on earth, more than three out of every four would be arthropods. Arthropods are the largest group of animals on earth.

There are five main kinds of arthropods, as you can see from their family tree above. Each kind is different, but all have some things alike:

1) Arthropods' legs have joints, so they bend
2) Arthropods' bodies have many sections (or 'segments')
3) Arthropods have exoskeletons—hard shells or skins on the outsides of their bodies

Colorado has animals from each of the five groups of arthropods. Some, like **CENTIPEDES**, you may not see too often, because they crawl around at night. Centipedes look like tiny worms with legs and flat bodies. **MILLIPEDE** means "thousand footed." They, too, look like worms with legs, but their bodies are round. Millipedes move slower than centipedes.

The bodies of both millipedes and centipedes are made up of tiny little sections. Centipedes have one pair of legs on each section; millipedes have two. "Centipede" means "hundred-footed," but the truth is, some have only 30 feet and some have more than 340 feet!

Since lobsters, shrimp and crabs are common **CRUSTACEANS**, you might think there are no crustaceans in Colorado. Wrong! We have crayfish and even some fresh water shrimp.

Crayfish (also called crawfish or crawdads) look like little lobsters, about three to six inches long. They make their homes in or near the water.

Colorado Division of Wildlife

In Louisiana, fishermen catch crayfish to use in soup and other food. But in Colorado and the rest of the U.S., crayfish are not often eaten.

INSECTS are the largest group of arthropods. Colorado itself has thousands of different kinds: ants, flies, mosquitoes, bees, butterflies, are just a few. All insects are alike in a few ways:

1) Insects' bodies have three sections
2) Insects' heads have two feelers (antennae) in front
3) Most insects have wings

One of Colorado's most famous insects is the grasshopper. Grasshoppers have a bad name in our state because they eat farmers' crops. There are two main kinds of grasshoppers: long-horned and short-horned. Long-horned hoppers have antennae that are longer than their bodies. Short-horned grasshoppers, sometimes called locusts, are the kind that farmers hate most.

Locusts migrate (move from one place to another) in large groups called swarms. Sometimes these swarms are so large they darken the sky like a cloud. Scientists say that one swarm in the Rockies had nearly 124 BILLION locusts. Just think how much grain all those grasshoppers could eat!

Most insects are much different now than when they first appeared on earth. But not cockroaches. They live now just as the first cockroaches did more than 300 million years ago. Cockroaches, too, have a bad name in Colorado. Most of the 2000 different kinds of cockroaches do not get in people's way. But the few who do will eat garbage, paper, clothes, books and many other things around the house. They live in warm, dark places.

ARACHNIDS—It is said that the Navajo Indians were the finest weavers in the world. Of them, Spider Woman wove the best. And where did Spider Woman learn to weave? From the Great Spider himself, the Navajos say.

Spiders live everywhere—from under the water to the highest mountain in the world. They are part of the group called arachnids (a-RAK-nids), along with ticks, mites, scorpions and more. Some are smaller than a pinhead. Others are as wide as a frisbee. The thousands of different kinds of spiders all have a few things that are alike:

1) Most spiders have eight legs and eight eyes
2) Most spiders' bodies have two segments
3) Spiders have no wings and no antennae
4) All spiders CAN build webs, but not all DO

Garden spiders weave the nicest webs. Chances are, when you see a web in some tall grass or in the corner of a window, it's an orb-weaver's web. Garden spiders belong to the orb-weaver family. Some orb weavers build a new web every night. Others just fix up the broken spots. No two webs are exactly alike!

Colorado has two kinds of poisonous spiders: the black widow and the brown recluse. You can tell a female black widow by the red hour-glass shape on her stomach. Black widows are shy; they set up their webs in dark, quiet places. Yes, a black widow's bite is poisonous. But in 200 years, only 55 people in Colorado are known to have been bitten by the black widow...and not one of them has died!

Think you've found a brown recluse? Look for a dark, violin-shaped mark on its back. If you want to get a little closer, count the number of eyes: a brown recluse has six; most other spiders have eight. Better be careful, now. A brown recluse bite can take weeks to heal and can leave an ugly scar. But before you get too worried, look up ''recluse'' in the dictionary to see why this spider got its name.

TICKS

One of the first things you should do when you get home from the mountains in the spring or summer is have someone check you for ticks. What you hope they don't find is a tiny, beetle-looking bug, about ¼ inch long, with a hard shell on its back. There are many kinds of ticks and they can cause many kinds of tick fever. In Colorado, the Rocky Mountain wood tick carries two nasty kinds of tick fever.

One kind is Rocky Mountain spotted fever. With this sickness, you can expect a high fever, chills, headache and red eyes. After a few days, you will get a red rash on your hands, which will spread over your whole body. But more likely, if you are bitten by a tick, you might get Colorado tick fever. This sickness is much like Rocky Mountain spotted fever, without the rash.

Colorado tick fever is the number one sickness in Colorado caused by arthropods' bites. There are about 100 cases every year. But before you come down too hard on ticks, black widows, rattlesnakes and other ''dangerous'' animals, ask yourself this: how many people die in car wrecks each year in Colorado?

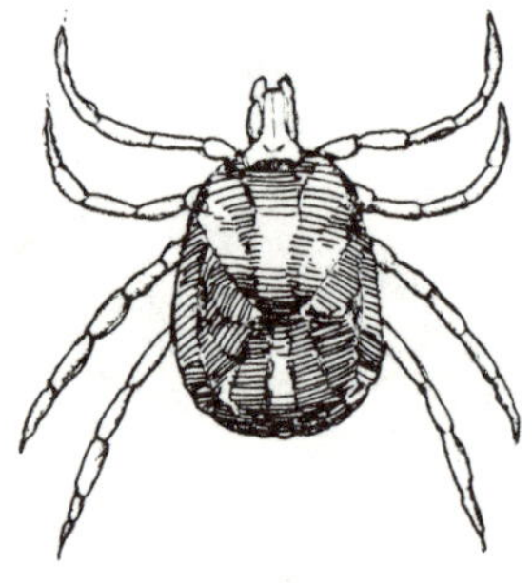

Want to avoid tick fever? 1) Stay out of places where there are many trees during the late Spring. 2) Before you go to the mountains, use a bug spray. It's hard to spray for ticks though, because they often crawl under your clothes and into your hair. 3) If you do find a tick, call a doctor right away to get it off, before it bites and starts to suck your blood. Just because you find a tick, doesn't mean you will get tick fever!

POINTS TO PONDER

1. One of Colorado's most famous naturalists was Theodore D.A. Cockerell. Dr. Cockerell was best-known for studying bees, but he also collected butterflies. Butterflies are insects with six legs and four wings. There are over 250 different kinds in Colorado, probably more than in any other state, so this is a great place to study them. There is a fine butterfly collection at the Denver Museum of Natural History. Call to find out when you can see it: (303) 575-3872.

2. SPIDERTRIVIA! Did you know.....

*A daddy-long-legs is not a spider. It belongs to the arachnid group, but it is not one of the spiders.

*The poorer a spider's eyesight, the better webs it will build!

*Colorado has tarantulas and they will bite, but they are not poisonous. A tarantula can live up to 25 years—pretty long for any bug! Tarantulas make good pets.

*A black widow gets it name because the female often (but not always) kills her mate.

*Spiders kill more insects than birds do!

*A jumping spider can jump 20-30 times as far as it is long. If you could do that, you could jump over 10 cars parked end to end in a line!

3. An arthropod museum? Yes, there is one right in Colorado, about eight miles southwest of Colorado Springs. There you can see more than 125 cases full of bugs and other arthropods. Call for a flyer or museum hours: May Natural History Museum (303) 576-0450.

4. Collecting insects can be a mighty interesting hobby. Where do you find them? How do you gather them? What do you do with them then? These books will help you get started on your bug collection:

Exploring the Insect World, by Margaret J. Anderson

The Bug Club Book: A Handbook for Young Bug Collectors, by Gladys Conklin

Insect Zoo, by Connie Ewbank

5. READ ON About Colorado's Bugs and other Arthropods. See if your library has these books:

Colorado Butterflies, by Brown, Eff and Rotger

Grasshoppers and Their Kin, by R. E. Hutchins

Guide to Some Common Colorado Spiders, by Walker Van Riper

Wildly Speaking, by M. B. Grant. Check the index under ants, grasshoppers, insects, monarch butterfly, tick.

BIRDS

One of the strangest sights in the ancient sky must have been the great flying reptiles. Big pieces of skin that stretched along their ''arms'' and ''legs'' allowed these creatures to fly. They flew, but they were not birds, for one very big reason: their ''wings'' did not have feathers. These flying reptiles were the early relatives of today's birds.

Scientists think the missing link came about 150 million years ago. This link was the archaeopteryx (ar-kee-OP-ter-ix), more like a reptile than a bird, for it still had teeth, claws and a tail like a reptile. But this new creature also had feathers, which made it our first real bird.

In the 150 million years since archaeopteryx, thousands of kinds of birds have come and gone from the earth. Today, scientists put all birds into 33 different groups or ''orders.'' Colorado has birds from 17 of these orders.

If you had a list of all the birds in each order, you would see that Colorado has more than 500 different kinds. Some of these are **residents**: they make their homes here. Residents stay all year; other birds for the summer or winter only. Still others just pass through Colorado from time to time. Many birds **migrate**: move from place to place. In the fall they move, looking for food for the winter. In the spring they move, looking for good places to lay their eggs and raise babies in the summer.

You can find some kinds of birds, like robins or red-winged blackbirds nearly anywhere in the U.S. But many birds are either ''eastern'' or ''western:'' they live either in the eastern or western U.S., but not both. The dividing line seems to be the Rocky Mountains, so in Colorado you can often see eastern birds as well as our own western birds.

With more than 500 different kinds of birds in Colorado, it's hard to know just where to begin your bird-watching. Let's pick one bird from each of Colorado's 17 orders and look at some interesting facts about that bird.

Colorado's Bird Orders

1. (ORDER: Loons)
COMMON LOON
Larger birds than ducks; can dive 200 feet. Have long, pointed bills. Bright, white spots on their backs in summer; spots very faint in winter.

2. (ORDER: Grebes)
WESTERN GREBE
Long necks, yellow beaks and red eyes. Often float nests in deep water. Sometimes eat their own feathers!

3. (ORDER: Pelicans, Cormorants, Darters)
DOUBLE-CRESTED CORMORANT
Look much like loons, but have hooked beaks, thin heads, orange throats and green eyes. This order small in Colorado.

4. (ORDER: Herons, Bitterns, Egrets, Ibises)
GREAT BLUE HERON
Stands four feet tall. Often called a crane by mistake. Largest long-legged bird in Colorado. Live in groups; make their nests in tall trees near the water.

5. (ORDER: Screamers, Swans, Geese and Ducks)
MALLARD
More mallards than any other Colorado waterbirds. Male has green head, reddish-orange feet.

6. (ORDER: Hawks, Kites, Eagles & Harriers)
RED-TAILED HAWK
Bird of prey: often given a bad name because they kill other animals for food, but very important to nature. Have large wings, and sharp, hooked beaks for tearing meat.

7. (ORDER: Grouse, Ptarmigan, Quail, Pheasant, Turkey)
SAGE GROUSE
Males sometimes spread tail feathers, puff out chests to show air sacs on neck; parade around and make popping sounds, "showing-off" for females.

8. (ORDER: Cranes, Rails, Coots)
VIRGINIA RAIL
Rails are secretive: more often heard than seen. Live in marshes. Can't fly well—go a short way and then land. Have long bills. Colorado's cranes are endangered.

9. (ORDER: Shore Birds, Gulls, etc.)
CALIFORNIA GULL
Many different families of birds in this order. Gull named Utah's state bird for saving early settlers' crops by eating millions of crickets. Mostly white, with green-ish legs and red eyelids.

10. (ORDER: Sand-grouse, Pigeons, Doves)
MOURNING DOVE
Very common, fast-flying birds that make low "coo-ing" noises. Mourning dove's coo is very sad, **mourn**ful. Have slim bodies with pointed tails; often found in cities.

11. (ORDER: Cuckoos & Roadrunners)
ROADRUNNER
Small order of long-tailed birds found mostly in southern Colorado. Like to race against horses or cars. Don't often fly. When they do, they go just a short way to tease other birds or animals, then land.

Jose Zamora
Alexander Wilson drawings from "American Ornithology"

Alexander Wilson drawings from "American Ornithology"

12. (ORDER: Owls)
GREAT HORNED OWL
Owls are birds of prey. Hunt mostly at night. This kind named for the little bunches of feathers on its ears.

13. (ORDER: Goatsuckers, Whip-poor-wills & Nighthawks)
COMMON NIGHTHAWK
Hunts at night—**nocturnal**. Likes to sit on fence posts and dead limbs, where its coloring makes it look like tree bark. Has a large mouth to catch insects while flying.

14. (ORDER: Hummingbirds & Swifts)
BROAD-TAILED HUMMINGBIRD
Hummingbirds are smallest birds in the world. Swifts are fastest flyers. Hummingbirds can fly backwards and hover (fly in one place). Eat one or two times their weight every day! Like to eat small insects and suck the nectar (sweet juice) from plants.

15. (ORDER: Kingfishers)
BELTED KINGFISHER
Gray-ish blue bird with crest on head. Eats mostly fish. Wings are long, strong and pointed; legs short and weak.

16. (ORDER: Woodpeckers, Flickers & Sapsuckers)
RED-SHAFTED FLICKER
Its strong beak hammers holes into trees. Its long, sticky tongue looks for bugs. 5000 ants once found in flicker's stomach. Most male birds in this order have some red on heads.

17. (ORDER: Perching Birds)
LARK BUNTING
Biggest of Colorado's bird orders. Most small birds that live on the land belong to this order. Order is so big that scientists have put perching birds into "families:" swallows, jays, wrens, starlings, waxwings and many more. Largest family is fringillidae (frin-JILL-a-day). Some birds in this family are grosbeaks, finches, sparrows, juncos, crossbills and buntings. In the bunting group, we find Colorado's state bird.

17.

There was much talk back in 1931 about which bird should be Colorado's state bird. Some people wanted the Meadowlark, but it was already state bird in many other places. The school children voted for the Mountain Bluebird. But when the lawmakers voted, they chose the Lark Bunting. Why? One story says that the government wanted to print the state bird on all of its stationery. Printing in color, of course, costs more than printing in black and white, so they chose the black and white Lark Bunting. Gee—They might have picked the Magpie!

Colorado Division of Wildlife

Since the Perching Birds are such a big order, let's look at a few other birds in that group that are quite common in Colorado:

MAGPIE

BLACK-BILLED MAGPIE—Not very well-liked because of some of its habits: eats eggs or babies from other birds' nests, attacks animals that are hurt or sick. But nothing is all bad—magpies eat grasshoppers and the bodies of dead animals, which helps clean up the land. Magpies have much longer tails than most Colorado birds.

GRAY JAY—Maybe this friendly, quiet, white-headed bird has come to your picnics in the mountains. Often called a "camp robber." A little higher in the mountains lives its "cousin," the beautiful deep blue **Stellar's Jay.** It has a high crown or **crest** on its black head.

MOUNTAIN BLUEBIRD—One of the prettiest Colorado birds. The male is a beautiful sky blue. Nearly chosen Colorado's state bird.

CEDAR WAXWING—Sometimes called "cherry birds" because they will pick a cherry and give it to another bird rather than eat it themselves. A group or **flock** of 10,000 cedar waxwings was once seen near the courthouse in Boulder.

CROSSBILLS—Named for the strange way their mouths close. There are five different kinds of crossbills in Colorado; most of them are partly red.

If you're a hunter, the chances are good that you're looking for birds from order number 7. Birds that are hunted are called **game birds.** Some of Colorado's best game birds are wild turkeys, chukar partridges, quail, grouse, mourning doves, band-tailed pigeons AND...

RING-NECKED PHEASANT—This very tasty bird is not a native. It was "introduced" or brought over from Asia. It's the most popular of Colorado's game birds.

WHITE-TAILED PTARMIGAN (TAR-me-gun: say "g" like girl)—This high mountain bird is one of the few that changes its coat. In winter, it's all white. As the snow melts and the rocks begin to show, it changes to brown and black. Ptarmigan have feathers on their feet down to their toenails, which act like snowshoes in the winter so they can walk on top of drifts.

Can you find the bird in this picture? How about the eggs? Like many animals, the ptarmigan is well-hidden or camouflaged (KAM-o-flajzd) because its coat blends in so well with the land around it.

Colorado Division of Wildlife

WHITE-TAILED PTARMIGAN

One order of Colorado birds is now **extinct**: Parrots and Parakeets. The Carolina Parakeet once lived in eastern Colorado and was seen in the early 1800's. Six kinds of Colorado birds are **endangered**: Greater Prairie Chicken, Prairie Sharp-tailed Grouse, Peregrine Falcon, Bald Eagle, Whooping Crane and Greater Sandhill Crane. And, if we're not careful, two more of our birds may soon be on this list: the Lesser Prairie Chicken and the White Pelican are now **threatened**. One of the biggest dangers to these birds is man. When man moves in, the birds move out. It is very important, if we are to keep birds off the extinct or endangered list, that we leave their wild areas wild.

POINTS TO PONDER

1. Colorado's best collection of mounted birds is at the Denver Museum of Natural History. Plan a visit to see for yourself how many different sizes, colors and shapes of birds there are in Colorado. Call to find out when you can see the birds: (303) 575-3872.

2. There is no way to tell in words just how each bird sounds. But there are some fine records with dozens of different bird sounds to help you tell their songs apart. Check your library for:

A Field Guide to Western Bird Songs
Songs of Western Birds: Record Album, Booklet
Song and Garden Birds of North America

3. One of the best places to bird-watch for both eastern and western birds is the South Platte Wildlife Area near Crook, Colorado. Run by the Colorado Division of Wildlife, this huge 22,000 acre space is the home for thousands of Colorado birds and visitors. If you live near Fort Collins, visit the Colorado Bird Refuge on the Poudre River at the very east end of town. Barr Lake, northeast of Denver and the Chatfield Recreation Area, southwest of Denver, are good bird-watching spots, too.

4. Why not keep a notebook of your favorite birds? Here are some things you might want to put in for each bird:

1. A colored picture of a male and female (since their colors can be quite different).
2. A feather.
3. A "menu" of what each bird eats.
4. Draw a picture of the bird's feet and beak. Did you know that you can often tell how a bird lives and what it eats just by looking at it? Birds with short, thick bills are probably seed-eaters. Hooked bills are for tearing meat. Flat bills are for scooping. If a bird's feet are webbed, it's probably a swimmer. If its toes have sharp hooks on the ends, it probably hunts fish or small animals. Look under "Birds" in the **Britannica Junior Encyclopedia** to find two nice picture charts with bird bills and feet.
5. Write a few sentences about any special body parts or strange habits of this bird.
6. Where does it live? What does its nest look like?
7. Draw a picture of the eggs.
8. Tell in your own words or jumble of letters, what sounds your bird makes.

5. **READ ON** About Colorado Birds. See if your library has these books:

Audubon Society Field Guide to North American Birds, Western Region (Alfred A. Knopf, publisher)

Birds of Colorado (2 volumes), by A.M. Bailey and R.J. Niedrach

Birds of Denver and Mountain Parks, by R. J. Niedrach and R. B. Rockwell

Birds of Rocky Mountain National Park, by Allegra Collister

Bird Memories of the Rockies, by Enos Mills

A Field Guide to Western Birds, by R. T. Peterson (goes with #2 above)

Game Birds of Colorado, by the Colorado Division of Wildlife

Pictorial Checklist of Colorado Birds, by A.M. Bailey and R.J. Niedrach

Wildly Speaking, by M. B. Grant (check the index for different bird types)

Kent & Donna Dannen

WILD FLOWERS

What would you say makes Colorado most different from other states? Probably the high mountains. When you think of high mountains, you think 'ice, snow, rocks, cold, wind.' But do you also think 'tiny, beautiful, wild flowers?' You should. Colorado's alpine wild flowers are some of the prettiest in the world.

Alpine wild flowers are tough (they have to be) but they are also delicate. It has taken them hundreds of years to get used to living in the cold, rocky land above timberline. Never pick or kill alpine flowers; they could take years (if **ever**) to grow back.

Most mountain wild flowers are small (dwarf) and they are perennials (purr-N-ee-uls). Perennial plants have strong roots or bulbs underground that help them live through the winter; not like annuals (AN-u-uls): plants that grow new from a seed and die each year.

One of the most beautiful high mountain flowers is the **alpine sunflower**. It looks like a dwarf of the big garden sunflower. As you may know, many plants follow the sun with their leaves or flowers. Alpine sunflowers don't. They always face east. So if you're lost above timberline, look for an alpine sunflower to help you find your way.

High mountain flowers come in pink, purple, red, yellow, green, blue, tan, white. Some bloom early, like the **alpine avens**, to tell that spring is coming. Others (like the **arctic gentian**) wait until August and early September, when most other plants have folded and winter is on its way. The **alpine forget-me-not** speaks for all the mountain plants. It makes us wonder how anything so small and beautiful could live in such a rough land.

Denver Botanic Gardens

About 350 million years ago, a big change took place in the plant world. Some kinds of plants began to make new plants from seeds instead of spores. The difference between spore plants and seed plants is a lot like the different between some egg-laying animals and mammals. **Spores** are left by the parent plant to grow as best they can, on the ground or in the water. But a **seed** plant keeps the seeds inside its body to grow for some time before they are put in the ground and sprout.

The very earliest plants, like animals, had only one cell and lived in the water, about 600 million years ago. Over millions of years plants changed, until some kinds were able to live on the land. Mosses, and much later, ferns, were the earliest kinds of land plants.

Most of today's flowers and plants are in the group called "Flowering and Fruiting Plants and Hardwood Trees." There are more than 125,000 different kinds in the world...2,000 right here in Colorado! Let's look at some of the groups or 'families' of wild flowers we most often find in Colorado. From each family, we will choose one or two special flowers to talk about.

Jane Kline

Common Colorado Plant Families

BUTTERCUP FAMILY

Some of the most beautiful and some of the most poisonous plants are in this family. Found in all life zones. A few plants in the buttercup family are: clematis, anemone, larkspur, buttercup and globeflower.

COLUMBINE

Colorado's state flower. Inside petals are white, outside a blueish-purple. High mountains have dwarf columbines: all purple. Southern Colorado has yellow; western slope, red and yellow. Columbine is protected by law: DO NOT PICK!

PASQUE FLOWER

"Pasqua" means 'Easter' in Spanish. Blooms near Easter-time. One of the best-loved flowers of the Rockies. Has a purple "cup" with yellow center.

CACTUS FAMILY

Barrel, pincushion and prickly-pear are all native Coloradans; HOWEVER, all but the prickly-pear are getting rare. Should not be picked or dug. Most live on plains; some in mountains. Cactus couldn't live in dry lands without spines—animals would chew them to suck the juice.

PRICKLY-PEAR

Many kinds of prickly-pear. Some have soft juicy fruits after the flowers fall off. Most have dry, hard fruits. Makes large yellow or red flowers.

COMPOSITE FAMILY

Largest of Colorado's plant families. Called 'composite' because many (100 or more) tiny flowers are bunched together on top of the plant to look like one flower. When you think of composites, think of dandelions or sunflowers. Some other composites are: yarrow, pussytoes, burdock, sagebrush, daisy, lettuce, ragwort, goldenrod, brown-(or black) eyed Susan.

ASTER

One of the prettiest wild flowers is the aster. Some have white flowers, some pink, but most common is purple. Found all over West, from plains to high mountains. A close look-alike is fleabane. DON'T MIX THEM UP!

THISTLE

YES: A thistle is a weed, but weeds have flowers too. Grows about 3 feet tall, with purplish (sometimes green or white) flower. Animals eat them in spite of prickles on stems and leaves. Another pretty weed is salsify. Looks like a big dandelion with its white "puff ball" when it goes to seed. Salsify's yellow flower stays open 'till 11 a.m., then closes for the day.

FIGWORT FAMILY

Figworts usually have tough stems and roots with flowers that look like little tubes. Some other figworts: foxglove, toadflax, monkey-flower, beard-tongue, mullein.

INDIAN PAINTBRUSH

Early summer is best time to see paintbrush. Yellow paintbrush of mountains found only in the Rockies. Down lower, paint-brush flowers are red and some-times even green.

Drawings by Barbara Tester

GENTIAN FAMILY

Some of the prettiest gentians are above timber-line. Most bloom in late summer. Many different kinds. Green gentians called 'monument plants' because they grow as tall as 6 feet! Rocky Mountain fringed gentian looks like a small purple iris. Flowers close up when it's cloudy.

Common Colorado Plant Families

HEATH FAMILY

Groups of heath plants are called heather. Usually a common mountain plant, but Colorado mountains are too dry for many kinds of heather. We have some laurel, blueberry, pipsissewa, etc., but our most common heather is

KINNIKINNICK

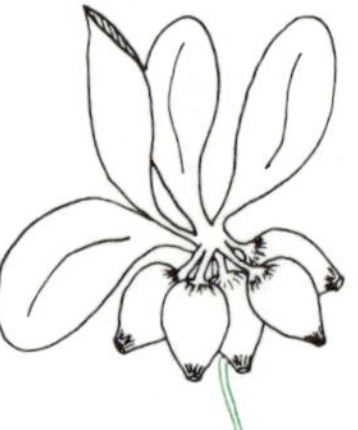

A 'ground cover' plant because it grows close to ground like a vine. Has shiny, 'waxy' leaves with pink and white flowers. In fall, flowers turn to bright red berries that bears love to eat. SO, often called bear-berries.

LILY FAMILY

If you're just learning about plants, lilies are great to study. They are built so that every part of the plant is easy to see. Scientists once put orchids, onions, asparagus and even yuccas into the lily family, because they are like lilies in many ways; but today these plants have their own families. The sand lily is one of Colorado's earliest and best-known spring flowers. Lilies grow from bulbs underground.

MUSTARD FAMILY

Plants in this family often used for food or medicine. (Ask your grandmother about making a mustard plaster for a chest cold.) Many mustards are garden vegetables: cabbage, cauliflower, turnip, brussels sprouts, etc.

WALLFLOWER

One of the prettiest wild plants of the mustard family is the wallflower. Flowers can be many shades of yellow. Found from plains to mountains. Named because they like to grow against rocks or walls.

MARIPOSA

'Mariposa' means 'butterfly' in Spanish. Mariposas often cover the flat tableland of Mesa Verde. Flower looks like a small, white tulip, but some kinds have flowers of yellow, orange, cream, pink, light purple, gray.

PEA FAMILY

Many plants that grow in "bad soil" (see Poisonous Plants Rule #9 on page 40) are from the pea family, the second largest family of seed plants. Many important food plants are peas. Garden beans and peas that people eat, clover and alfalfa that animals eat are in the pea family. Even the locust tree is a pea! More than 150 plants of the pea family are native Coloradans. Some common wild peas are wild liquorice, vetch, peavine, lupine, golden banner AND:

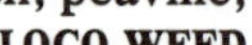

LOCO-WEED

The loco-weed is seen mostly on plains; sometimes in mountains. About a foot tall with flowers shaped like flower garden sweet peas. Can be white, cream, pink or purple. 'Loco' means 'crazy' in Spanish. Horses won't eat it unless they can't find other food; but once they try it, they're "hooked." They eat more and more. At first they get tired; then wild and crazy. Finally they begin losing weight until they die.

CLOVER

Clover is one of the most healthful foods for wild animals; has lots of protein. Deer and elk eat clover, too, not just cows and horses. The deer clover (not shown here) grows in thick clumps on rocky places in the high mountains. Called a "cushion plant" because it feels like a thick rug when you step on it...sort of 'springy.'

Drawings by Barbara Tester

ROSE FAMILY

This family has some of the best wild foods: strawberries, raspberries and cherries are roses. Also makes a nice plant for lawns and gardens. Rose parts often used for medicine (look for rose hips in the drug store sometime).

SHRUBBY CINQUEFOIL

In French, cinquefoil means "five leaves," but most Colorado cinquefoils have more than five parts to their leaves. As its name says, this wild rose grows in clumps like a shrub. Blooms all summer long with pretty yellow flowers. Makes a nice bush for the lawn, but don't dig up the wild ones. Buy your lawn bushes at a greenhouse. Usually wild plants will not live if you transplant them (move them to a different place). This rose has no thorns. Keeps its leaves all winter.

POINTS TO PONDER

1. You can see plants from Colorado and from all over the world at the Denver Botanic Gardens. There are indoor gardens, outdoor gardens and special shows all year round. Call or write to learn more about what you can see and when: Denver Botanic Gardens; 909 York Street; Denver, CO 80206   (303) 575-3751

2. Making a flower collection can be great fun. The book **Rocky Mountain Flora,** by Wm. A. Weber (pages 15-17), tells you how to make a collection of dried or pressed flowers. But before you pick real flowers, COUNT! Are there more than five of these flowers in a five-foot area? If there are, you make take ONE. Remember, many flowers (especially alpine wild flowers) take years to come back, if ever. NEVER pick alpine wild flowers, columbine or rare flowers. (Any guidebook will tell you which wild flowers are rare.) For this part of your collection, take along your camera and bring home a picture instead of a flower.

3. Here are the names of some other common Colorado plant families. Unscramble the circled letters to spell the name of a pretty bluc Colorado wild flower. (HINTS: This flower belongs to the buttercup family. It can be poisonous. A town between Denver and Colorado Springs has the same name.)

B U C K W H E A T   P H L O X   O R C H I D
E V E N I N G   P R I M R O S E   S A X I F R A G E
P U R S L A N E   P R I M R O S E

____ ___ ___ ____ ____ ___ ____ ____ ___

4. **READ ON** About Colorado Wild Flowers. See if your library has these books:

Colorado Mushrooms, by M. H. Wells and D. H. Mitchel

Colorado West, Land of Geology and Wildflowers, by R. G. and J. W. Young

Colorado Wild Flowers, by Harold and Rhoda Roberts

Edible Native Plants of the Rocky Mountains, by H. D. Harrington

A Field Guide to Rocky Mountain Wildflowers, Craighead, Craighead and Davis

Handbook of Rocky Mountain Plants, by R. A. Nelson

Kinnikinnick: The Mountain Flower Book, by Millie Miller

Meet the Natives, by M. Walter Pesman

Mountain Wild Flowers of Colorado, by Ruth Nelson and Rhoda Roberts

Potions, Portions, Poisons, by G. S. Cutts

Rocky Mountain Wildflowers, by Kent and Donna Dannen

LOVELY TO LOOK AT, DELIGHTFUL TO EAT (?!*?)

* EDIBLE AND MEDICINAL PLANTS *

If you like corn on the cob, you might also want to try cattail on the cob! Oh, perhaps you didn't know—cattails (those tall plants with the brown tube-like tops that grow in swampy places) make some of the best wild food.

But maybe you're feeling a little sick instead; might be coming down with the flu. What you need are some wild onions. For coughs, drink onion juice mixed with honey. Or if you're just feeling all-around awful, try what the Indians did: "Cover the body with ground onions, wrap up well and sweat."

Before you try using wild flowers for food or medicine, you should know them very well. Often there is very little difference between a plant that might cure you and a plant that might kill you. Here are some rules to remember:

Poisonous Plant Rules

1. Just because animals eat the flowers or berries doesn't mean you can! Animals *usually* do not eat poisonous plants, but if they're hungry enough, they will.

2. The whole plant may be poisonous, or just certain parts may be poisonous. Water hemlock, the most poisonous plant in this part of the world, has most of its poison in its lower stems or roots. But it's best to eat NO PART of a poisonous plant.

3. Some plants are poisonous just at certain times of the year. *Young* skunk cabbage seems to be poisonous to animals, but they sometimes eat older skunk cabbage. People should NEVER eat it.

4. Cooking *may* get rid of some or all of the poison, but it may *not*, too! Indians would eat the roots and leaves of lupine IF it had been cooked, but please, don't you try it.

5. Never guess that a plant is safe to eat just because it looks like another plant that is safe. Dogbane, a poisonous plant, looks a lot like the very tasty milkweed, which is OK to eat after cooking.

6. Right in the same family, one kind of plant may be good to eat while another is poisonous. Some kinds of milkweed make very good food; other kinds are poisonous.

7. White and red berries are often more dangerous than blue or black ones, but be very sure of any berry before you eat it. The Western Baneberry with its pretty red or white berries is quite poisonous.

8. Stay away from all mushrooms and toadstools unless you're an expert. It takes only one of a kind called the "death angel" to kill you.

9. Some kinds of plants are poisonous only when they're growing in a certain kind of dirt. A few plants will grow *only* in this "bad dirt." Milkvetch is one of these plants. When you see milkvetch, you know that all the plants around it are growing in this bad dirt, SO DON'T EAT ANY OF THEM!!!

10. Even when you're sure a plant is safe, eat only little bits at a time. If you HAVE made a mistake, it's better to have eaten just a little. The Rocky Mountain iris tastes sweet at first and you might want to eat a lot, but later it causes a bad burning in the mouth and throat.

Big Stump at Florissant Fossil Beds

TREES, SHRUBS AND GRASSES

MAY 18, 1980—The shock from the blast blew down 44,000 acres of evergreen trees. Heat killed millions of fish in the rivers. More than 1,000 feet of the mountain was blown right off! Ash seven inches deep was found in many nearby states. This was the famous volcano, Mt. St. Helens in Washington.

But 35 million years ago, the same kind of thing was happening right here in Colorado. Just west of what is now Colorado Springs was Lake Florissant (FLOR-is-sunt). Near the lake lived many kinds of plants and animals that you would never find there now. Colorado was much warmer and wetter then, not as high as it is today. Large ferns and palm trees grew near the lake. There were HUGE redwood trees like you might now find in California.

There were also volcanoes near the lake, and they erupted (blew up) just like Mt. St. Helens. Birds and larger animals could get away from the erupting volcanoes. But when the thick ash settled on Lake Florissant, it trapped many insects and plants. Each eruption put another layer of ash over the trees, insects and plants, sealing them off from the weather. Without the wind, rain and sun, plant and animal fossils stayed just as they were, for millions of years. It wasn't until 1874 that scientists found what they now call "the most beautiful and detailed fossils of this kind in the world." So far, 80,000 fossils of ancient palm leaves, evergreen needles, redwood stumps, butterflies, spiders, fish and other early life have been found at the Florissant Fossil Beds.

Today, Colorado being higher and drier, the palms and giant redwoods can no longer grow here. Let's look at some of the trees, shrubs and grasses that are "native" (grow wild) in Colorado today. Unlike many plants that have been brought here from other places, natives know how to live in Colorado's thin, dry air, with its lack of water and its hard winter storms.

SOME COLORADO NATIVES

FIR & SPRUCE TREES

Both are part of pine family. Fir and spruce are hard to tell apart. Three clues: 1) Spruce cones hang down; fir sit up on branch. 2) Spruce has prickly needles; fir are soft. 3) When needles fall off spruces, the bare twigs are rough or bumpy; bare fir twigs are smooth. All fir and spruce trees are evergreens, with cones and needles.

COLORADO FIR TREES:
Alpine, White, Douglas (this is the most popular western Christmas tree)

COLORADO SPRUCE TREES:
Englemann, Colorado Blue

COLORADO
STATE
TREE

COLORADO BLUE SPRUCE
A beautiful evergreen, found near streams. Needles are green to silvery gray, but look blue when grouped together on the tree. Named state tree in 1939.

JUNIPERS
Can be either trees or shrubs, depending on where they live. Taller "trees" are Utah, Colorado, Rocky Mountain juniper and some cedar trees. Cones are small and packed so tight they look like berries. Cherry-stone, Low and One-seed are some "shrub" junipers. Berries are often blue.

Colorado Historical Society

SHRUB OR TREE???

Isn't an oak a tree? Aren't willows, elders and birches trees, too! Now junipers and pinon pines, they're shrubs, right? And what about fruit trees like cherry and plum—some look like trees and some look like shrubs! The answer is this: some plants can be either shrubs or trees. *Usually* a plant that is more than 20 feet high is a tree. A tree *usually* has one main stem (trunk). A shrub is *usually* less than 20 feet and has many smaller stems (or trunks) where it comes out of the ground. A plant's habitat sometimes tells which it will be. Often a plant that is a tree in the foothills or montane zones will be smaller in the thin air of timberline. Then it becomes a shrub. When many shrubs grow close together, you have a bush!

Dr. Jim Feu

SCRUB OAK
Can be either a tree or shrub. Smallest are about four feet tall, but may get as high as 35 feet. Many different kinds of scrub oak, but like all oaks, these plants make acorns. "Mighty oaks from little acorns grow"... (Or is it "Mighty aches from little toe corns grow"???)

Colorado Historical Society

DECIDUOUS (d-SID-you-us) OR EVERGREEN???

A deciduous tree or shrub drops its leaves every year, all at the same time. An evergreen stays green all year. It does shed, but not all at once. Old leaves or needles fall off *after* the new ones have grown. DON'T BE FOOLED! Not all evergreens look like pine trees. Some evergreens have leaves, not needles; and some make berries, not cones!

SAGEBRUSH
Big Sagebrush is Colorado's most common sage. Has a nice, strong smell when fresh, but STINKS when burned. Can usually tell how good the ground is by how tall the sagebrush grows.

American plum, wild red raspberry, myrtle blueberry, golden currant, thimbleberry, gooseberry, western chokecherry, sand cherry, billberry...this is just a start. Did you ever dream Colorado had so many wild treats?

COLORADO'S PRETTIEST SHRUB?
Just maybe! By far, one of the most colorful shrubs of the Rocky Mountains. Has bright red stems and white berries, which make good food for birds and mammals. Indians used stems for making baskets. Now often used as a lawn shrub. Other natives which make nice lawn shrubs are mountain mahogany, western chokecherry, Rocky Mountain sumac.

Dr. Jim Feucht

COLORADO REDOSIER DOGWOOD

A large family of evergreens. Needles of most pines longer than other evergreens. Turpentine made from some kinds of pines. Colorado's common pines are pinon, lodgepole, ponderosa. Limber pines are the largest Colorado evergreens and make the largest cones. Bristlecone pines are the short, twisted trees of the high mountains.

LODGEPOLE PINE
Almost always found in montane zone. Cones open only when warm. Love sun; grow straight and tall, with few branches on lower trunk. Named because Indians used the tall, straight limbs and trunks for building lodges and teepees.

PONDEROSA PINE
The most common evergreen tree of the foothills. Not 'cone-shaped' with needles from top to bottom like many pines, spruces and firs. Easy to see trunk and branches on lower part of tree. Mistletoe (which can kill a tree) often grows on ponderosas.

PINON PINE
A small pine with small cones. Needles are short, with white line on inside. Lives mostly in the plains and foothills zones, usually in southern Colorado. Nuts inside the cones are very good to eat.

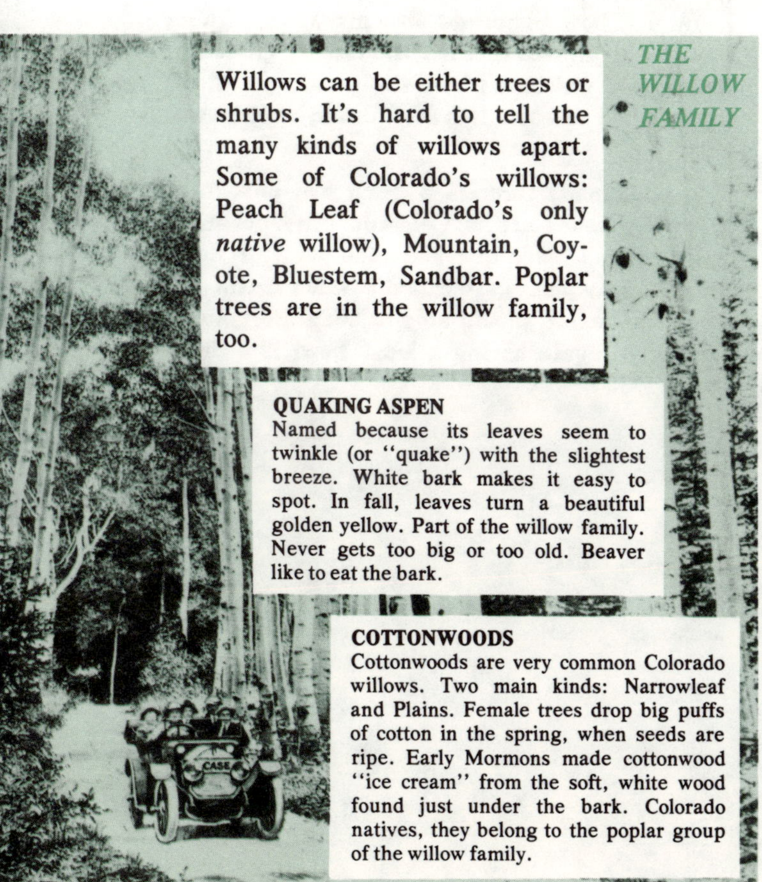

Willows can be either trees or shrubs. It's hard to tell the many kinds of willows apart. Some of Colorado's willows: Peach Leaf (Colorado's only *native* willow), Mountain, Coyote, Bluestem, Sandbar. Poplar trees are in the willow family, too.

THE WILLOW FAMILY

QUAKING ASPEN
Named because its leaves seem to twinkle (or "quake") with the slightest breeze. White bark makes it easy to spot. In fall, leaves turn a beautiful golden yellow. Part of the willow family. Never gets too big or too old. Beaver like to eat the bark.

COTTONWOODS
Cottonwoods are very common Colorado willows. Two main kinds: Narrowleaf and Plains. Female trees drop big puffs of cotton in the spring, when seeds are ripe. Early Mormons made cottonwood "ice cream" from the soft, white wood found just under the bark. Colorado natives, they belong to the poplar group of the willow family.

Colorado Historical Society

For many people in eastern Colorado, the 1930's were the "Dirty Thirties" or the "Dust Bowl" years. Off and on for 10 years, great clouds of dirt filled the air. Sometimes the dust clouds were so dark, it looked like night. Sand piled up like snowdrifts. Farmers and ranchers lost their crops and moved away.

What caused the Dust Bowl? Very little rain, for one thing. Wind, for another. But one of the biggest reasons was lack of grass.

Many early farmers on the Plains had plowed up the buffalo grass and other native grass to plant their crops. Ranchers had let their animals eat too much of the Plains grass, until there was none left in many places. They didn't know just how important this grass was. The roots of the grasses reached into the dry ground, looking for water. Without the grass, the dirt (or soil) had no roots to hold it down, so it blew away.

Too late, many farmers learned just how important grasses are to Colorado. The government started plans to replant the grass. Today these grassy places are called "National Grasslands." Grasses should help to keep the Plains from ever again having a Dust Bowl like that in the 1930's.

BUFFALO GRASS

More than 80 different kinds of grasses grow on the eastern Colorado Plains: Wheat-grass, Bent-grass, Big Bluestem, Foxtail, Oat-grass, Grama, Fescue, Muhly, Needle-grass are just a few. One of the easiest grasses to grow in Colorado is Buffalo grass. This native can stand Colorado's strong winds and hot sun. Needs little rain. Grows about four inches tall.

POINTS TO PONDER

1. Would you like to see one of Colorado's giant redwood stumps, left over from 35 million years ago? Take the "Big Stump" tour at the Florissant Fossil Beds, between Colorado Springs and Cripple Creek. At Florissant you can also look through strong glasses at the insect, fish and leaf fossils. If you can't visit, write for a free flyer:

Florissant Fossil Beds National Monument
P.O. Box 185 Florissant, CO 80816

2. One of the oldest living things on earth may be the small, wind-blown-looking trees near timberline. Scientists have found bristle-cone pines that are 4,600 years old! How can they tell? Each year, most trees grow a new layer of wood called a "ring." When the tree is cut, you can count the rings to tell how old the tree is. In dry years, the rings will be thin; in wet years, wider. Each ring = one year. Next time you see a tree stump, count the rings to tell its age.

3. Colorado has two National Grasslands, set up by the government, where you can drive, hike, camp or picnic. At first, all you see is mile after mile of low hills covered with grass. But stop to think what happened when this grass wasn't here! Then look around for wildlife. You'll see many different kinds of grasses, wild flowers, birds, small mammals and snakes. If you can't visit the Grasslands, write for maps and flyers which will tell you more about them:

Pawnee National Grassland
2009 9th Street
Greeley, CO 80631

Comanche National Grassland
Carrizo Ranger District
212 E. 10th Street/P.O. Box 127
Springfield, CO 81073

4. In Denver, you can take a self-guided tour of many Colorado trees. Fairmount Cemetery (East Alameda and South Quebec) has a walking tour which points out 19 famous Colorado trees. The cemetery sells a book called **Trail of Trees** which tells about each tree and a little of its history in Colorado.

5. **READ ON** About Colorado's Trees, Shrubs and Grasses. See if your library has these books:

Colorado Evergreens, by R. E. More

Grow Native, by S. Huddleston and M. Hussey

A Guide to the Woody Plants of Colorado, by G. W. Kelly

Meet the Natives, by M. W. Pesman

Rocky Mountain Flora, by W. A. Weber

Rocky Mountain Trees, by R. J. Preston, Jr.

Shrubs for the Rocky Mountains, by G. W. Kelly

Trees for the Rocky Mountains, by G. W. Kelly